In Life

Acknowledgements: The translator would like to thank Gian Lombardo for his editorial acumen and belief in this work. Thanks also to David Wills, Hannah Freed-Thall and Cole Swensen for their perceptive feedback and guidance. Finally, thanks are given to Eugène Savitzkaya for his insights and his words.

This translation was made possible by support from Service de la Promotion des Lettres, Belgian Ministry of Culture.

FÉDÉRATION
WALLONIE-BRUXELLES

Cover: *Flowers and Vegetables (Fleurs et legumes)*, by James Ensor, 1896, oil on canvas, 121.5 x 101.5 cm, Ernest Rousseau Collection, Brussels, Koninklijk Museum Voor Schone Kunsten, courtesy Lukas-Art in Flanders VZW, photo by Hugo Maertens. Additional copyrights SABAM Belgium.

ISBN: 978–1–935835-23-3 trade paperback edition

LCCN: 2018954848

Quale Press
www.quale.com

In Life

a novella by

Eugène Savitzkaya

Translated from the French by Andrew Colpitts

Quale Press

IN THIS HOUSE only the latch gleams—the latch on the front door. The faucet drips incessantly. The doors open at the slightest breeze. The rain has rotted the weathering on most of the windows. Water seeps in through cracks in the foundation. Ever-extending fissures have torn the wallpaper carefully hung on the chalky, waxen walls. With each gust of wind, dust falls from the attic above. The metal frame for the awning is thoroughly rusted and bent. One by one the windowpanes will shatter—I guarantee you that. All the doors are broken, missing or off-kilter, letting cold air and light pass through. Are the hinges misaligned? Has the wood warped? It all happened at the same time, each element working independently, bricks weighing on lintels, lintels weighing on bricks and wood-work, woodwork spitting out its pegs and dislodging the scrap metal it's riddled with, bricks split, rain flowing drop by drop into the cracks, a gathering of fungi, cloud of spores, breeding ground for shipworms, ruins of tun-nels and ancient coal pits—all one work realized in the emptiness of forgetting what should go without saying in the crevices of a house poorly dovetailed in thought.

On the other hand, the rooms are spacious and the floors level, or nearly. A little bit of air and a little bit of sun make life possible. A little bit of stubbornness as well.

Only the latch gleams, the latch on the main door. The peach trees have leaf curl and the apple trees, fire blight. There's white mold everywhere. The aphid popu-lation is exploding. Worms inhabit the blue plum tree. Sap dribbles from the feet of the cherry trees. On the ground, moss suffocates grass. There's no money to make any drastic changes.

We carry on washing the windows of the dirty, dusty house and carry on waxing the woodwork.

It came to pass that, gradually, time crept out of the house, our home; no more watches, neither on my fiancée's wrist nor my own; no more clocks—the last, battery powered, died just now, on this Thursday afternoon of this hazy October when the air brusquely soured in the broad hollowness of time. We'd been warned about it, given the way we'd begun to live, here, in the house on Rue Chevaufosse, the old hillside path. We'd begun to trust in the sound of the city and in our own warmth.

Every Saturday, if I were to write a love letter, here's how I'd begin: Why have you abandoned me? Here I am now with a bowl of red berries in my hand for you. I gathered them in the garden where I'll never be gardener, or maybe an exceedingly discreet gardener, always grumpy in his good humor. We hear the saw's sad voice as it enters the wood without playing the game, cheating, cheating, taking shortcuts, growing away from the heart by whittling it down bit by bit.

This Thursday, a strange a Thursday as Thursdays can be, a Thursday that I'll never forget as I never forget any Thursday, any Tuesday, any Friday, any Monday, any Saturday, any Sunday and especially any Wednesday. This Thursday, I made it. I put all the apples from one tree in one basket. But it wasn't an aroma of apples that reigned in the garden. It was more subtle still.

What a shock we had when we noticed that all the water we had used up over such a long time had not flowed far from us, but had accumulated somewhere in a hidden dry well in the garden! It's a good thing that thick sandstone pipes dispatch the family crap to the big communal collectors. It's helpful to know by heart the precise pathways that these precious channels follow. It's unwise to live in complete ignorance of channelization. In these buried and forgotten pipes there's a kind of clogging of collective history and personal memory. But it's beyond time, in oblivion, far from the light, where the famous foxtail amaranth forms. On Saturday, I was wont to pull a handsome specimen from the least overrun section of the system. The shrewd and sly fox had surely passed by there and left a conspicuous sign of his finest ruse—a blockage measuring three feet long, a natural obstacle to the sewage flow, having become (in a hundred years or more) impregnable. Having lived in the hope of extraordinary events, we'd forgotten ourselves and in this oversight—the void of this oversight—the right order of things becomes self-evident, the unheeded roots grow at a quickened pace and break through the pipes, dams form, turning back the flow of time. Something reverses, turns upon itself. It was only when the odor of shit rose from the dry well that we knew what, for a hundred years, we'd left beneath our feet.

There's a doormat whose use is plain and simple. In summer, it's perfectly enjoyable as a pillow, the rest of the body putting up with the hardness of the concrete. Two cats have already died on this humble litter. It will be burnt in the first fire of spring or else devoured by the flames where we throw dead wood, dismantled crates and various scraps before winter's arrival. In winter, sodden with water, it freezes and becomes an (indecipherable) tablet. We shake it out when it's soaked. A doormat is never eternal. It sometimes seems vile, vaguely in our image. It stinks. What was it again that spattered it with vomit? It always elicits the weightiest questions: Who are we to leave such traces?

I need two pairs of hands. One for household chores, the other for writing. It's so unpleasant to touch paper with dry, battered hands. And it's even less pleasant to pull buttercups and touch black earth with hands gloved in felt or leather. Yet the two types of work seem necessary and inseparable, like lighting a fire in the wood stove and emptying it of the ashes that choke it. The same hands accomplish all tasks. They cut and transport the wood, light the fire in the stove and, benefitting from the warmth of the room, handle paper. I work the wheel and the mill at the same time. The same hands serve for everything and make every part of the world commune together—dirt with stomach, mouth with anus, plate with toilet bowl and the alphabet with the heart of wood. The same inimitable hands maneuver helpful shortcuts between the tempered steel sewing needle (for sewing buttons back on again) and the attentive eye of others. It's fair that they should be arbiters and suffer a bit—they who have access to firesides' warmth, to smoothness, to silk, to unfamiliar skin.

I must jot down some words, but here I am having to search for Louise's slippers, and here I am roaming the house since it proves necessary to look under the furniture, where you can discover the most beautiful, commonplace objects, those whose need is forever felt. I would like a spoon soft against lips and yet which must be mistrusted because of a tiny, sharp notch that the tongue cannot help but search for: there it is. I would like the marble that seems to hold a flame and a wisp of smoke: there it is. Here's where all treasures have been buried. Here's where the search must start for what-have-you and, of course, Louisette's slippers, and what's missing from the dresser, workbench, library, medicine cabinet and, of course, memory. These places, more or less plentiful depending on the house's layout, more or less kept up, act as an anteroom, a purgatory, an accidental hiding place. They revive our most worn principles, returning objects to their original nature and giving them a new season of use. They constitute too, of course, an airlock before total oblivion, before total loss. But when most of the usual places have been checked, you have to get on all fours and look under the furniture, in the pockets of armchairs, behind the baseboard and in between floorboards. The gold growing there is worth as much as sand—that's to say an incalculable worth.

On Thursday, I don't wash my hands—not even once, neither morning nor night. What's the point? And I go to bed with my sticky hands that have touched the worm-eaten, fat, the damp, fragrant oil and saliva. They smell of garlic, celery, smoke, curdled milk and, of course, carrion. They're stained from red cabbage and soot. I reject them. I don't like them. They weigh me down. They've worked too much and I banish them from me. I find them too cold and too rough. And yet, I know that I'm compelled to reconcile with them. A bath will be a fine reconciliation. Little by little, as the day carries on, the disintegration of my body becomes ever more marked. Pieces threaten to fall off. Entire sections rupture. I have forgotten my mother and I launch a useless and draining struggle against my father. I exert so little influence over my limbs that all the blood in them flows toward the ground. I'm worried. The flourishing bindweed has cut my work out for me.

The children, adorned with garlands of flowered bindweed, have on this tranquil Tuesday decorated the garden with a fort they've built fills that it from wall to wall. Now the bindweed arrays in the children's hair, and its flowers rim their eyes, highlighting their sparkle and resolve.

Children are but in dreams, standing next to a wain full of hay, pulling a straw-colored pony by the bridle, or sitting in a propellerless plane smack dab in the middle of Saint-Lambert's Square, all blue with pigeons from before the flood and plagues. The footbridges spanning deep silted rivers were crossed in one nimble bound. They're the sort of slow rivers of places bearing names as strange as Petit-Axhe, Grand-Axhe or Cras-Avernas. And baths were taken in good company.

If morning bath is a lark, evening bath is a solemn act. In the morning, you get your blood pumping, you pinch yourself (it's a matter of checking for usual consistency and a certain vitality), and you rinse out the rheum and the sleep from your eyes. Even if the work of regaining your spirits, of standing yourself up and holding yourself in that pose is sometimes slow and grueling, you know that you're coming back to life, that a new day is ahead, that a surplus of hours is once again granted, a surplus we can neither hold nor save, like a fist of gold pieces that need to be spent before they reveal their elementary nature: sand. My morning bath is a host of sprinklings, of fine droplets, a series of crises and solemnities. We stopped, it seems, being children and now have to embark on the sanitary habits of the old. There is no middle ground. With evening bath we prepare for sleep. Feet must be void of all roughness in order to climb into the tipsy ship in relentless distress, and clean to tread on the white canvas. In darkness, we grope along to hold tight to the ship and we feel more at ease with smooth feet and clear ears. The hours we had been granted have silenced themselves forever—we have consumed too much food, breathed too much air. Why such greed? Moreover evening bath is at once a reconciliation with the various elements that compose us and a childish respite—oh so soft—from the losses and disasters of the day. Tomorrow will be Monday.

There is, on this rainy Monday, a little girl who touches everything, passing her hand over every object, ruffling feathers to see whether the plumage will return to its unruffled state. And there's another little girl who watches. And there's a little boy who watches the two little girls. The story starts and multiplies its characters, for it's raining and, as everyone knows, rain multiplies appearances. There came a day when the little girls who touch everything lifted up the most incongruous objects as if to weigh their meaning. They lifted up truck tires that they immediately dropped, with the tires bursting into flame. They lifted telephone poles, which they dropped and the poles broke irreparably into pieces. The irreparable came early. They twirled the statue of Charlemagne on a horse and toppled it with an intolerable din. The intolerable had driven back the borders of the intolerable. They suddenly caught a snake who seemed stiff on the outside, but changed form thirty times before wrapping round the ankles of the little girls, leaving a light ring. The little girls, watching intently, watched the fire flaring black with endless opaque smoke. They watched the bits of telephone poles that first rolled left, then rolled to the right of the broken axle. They watched Charlemagne's horse, showing a different flank in the pallid light, and, with their foot, they rolled the serpent into a ball and pushed it away. The little boys who had helped in all these marvels neither did nor said anything for they were so flabbergasted, but when the time came they threw themselves into a sudden stampede, kicking and pawing the ground without cease. And the world was born.

The children, armed with privet sticks, drenched in muddy water, carried out hurried baptisms. These great destroyers of Saturday trees, on Sunday will they tear down the wall that struggles to hold back the boxwood roots whose branches must, sooner or later, be sawed off?

I'm partial to the saw. I pull the saw and the saw drags me along me as casually as if I'd shared a ton of salt with it. The times when I saw day-long I must have the same face as the saw, a clear face—sullen, stubborn and detached. I go back and forth in the company of the saw and I set aside from these travels only the memory of the pale light that I didn't even think fit to discern. I saw facing the face of the clock and through rays of sunlight. The saw, with its gleaming and finely shaped blade, builds a white path in daylight and I plunge myself into it. Will I accomplish some pious deed? The beams I erected in the garden I have now returned to the shed. To put them into the shed I must cut them into pieces so they can fit in the stove that will consume them, warming me so I can write, read and draw with chalk. I should say for clarity's sake I have the saw in my blood and it steers me where it wants for I'm hypnotized by it. I saw and slice through resin and between knots. I dismantle the ancient cohesion of wood. Oh, how I hate to stink.

I sweep the sawdust I sow. I rake the leaves of the trees I planted and let grow. I pick up pigeon shit I tolerate. I wash the windows my steam fogs. I shake out the doormat I muddy. I clean the plate I dirty. I empty the ashtray I fill. I wash away the sweat I secrete. I clear the toilet I clog. I make the bed I've slept in. And I start over each day. Nothing governs me and no one reigns over my life.

Does there exist so great a pleasure as washing the windows of a veranda flooded with evening sunlight? When I wash the windows of the sunny veranda, I am the acrobat of glass, happily working so the light enters the house

14

wave by wave. In a way, I polish these rays of sunshine, I comb them, I arrange them. I bathe the light itself, like a mother would her children, and I bathe it with great care and such tenderness, bearing in mind its fragility as much as its vitality. I give it a reinvigorating bath of white vinegar in the sharp and soft light. But no matter how I try, impurities, clouds, signs of oxidation, aging and the day's etiolation persist. But I continue and strive to dissolve the membrane that forever separates me from the sun. I quickly renounce purity and perfection, promising myself to routinely combat that ever-expanding opacity with everything I've got: a pail of vinegar water, a sponge, a chamois cloth and a scrap of linen.

To clean glasses, dunk them in soapy water. They dissolve to reappear in light's purity, humble and pious vials that can once again hold syrupy milk, weak wine and water thicker than blood. The best way to wash plates and platters is to slather them with slightly sandy dirt then rinse the enamel with fresh water. Having said this, the dishes, immediately following a meal, no matter what, compose a great assortment of clattering, clonks and sloshing that is almost always as melodious and soothing for those resting as for those bustling about. It's essential to complete this task immediately following the meal so as to save oneself from the violent and entirely antidigestive sight of the flagrant corruption of an enchantment. We are compelled to eliminate the creaminess and the flavors before they begin to smell, blacken and dry. This task can only fall upon one of the diners who dodges this disaster in the twinkling of an eye. You must return to a limbo so you can give yourself the chance to prepare a new feast. After each meal, I wash the dishes in the hope of delaying the moment of the decomposition of flesh and grace. First, I wash the glasses, then the plates, the knives, the spoons and the forks and, finally, the pots and pans in which everything was cooked, on metal or clay where the revelation took place, foretelling an irrevocable rot. I cooked rice, asparagus and chicken to tenderize them, extract the aroma and render the flavor more human. Now the crumbs are under the table. Who will sweep them up?

We sweep and wash the floor to erase the traces of our passage, the traces of feasts, and to fight in vain against the dust from the outside that rides in on the wind, on light and on soles. We fight, too, against the slag of what's crumbling inside, bit by bit, under our feet and between our fingers and, bit by bit, by tiny shovelfuls, we rid ourselves of what we possess—paper, furniture, walls, hair and our skin. It's best not to sort scraps, risking endless work, disgust and gloom. We must throw stuff away without thinking. We could believe, having seen the crumbs collected under the broom, that it would be easy, what with so many tiny, varied pieces, to reconstruct a sort of homunculus capable of gesticualting, lively and kind, but it's only a question of waste. But notice how at the moment you slide the little pile from the metal dustpan, a pearl, a little watch, the precious screw from a pencil sharpener or an indispensible spring clinks. With time passing, the children of the house, Marin and Louise, permit some sacrifices with regard to the house itself. Notice then how useful it is to group peels before sending them to hell. For that matter, this is how we find all lost buttons, almost every key and those dangerous shards of glass. This is how we form the necessary chronicle of bygone days and draw up a list of what no longer belongs to us.

You must fight against the vacuum cleaner that sucks away the precious fragments of your life, that would have you believe that yesterday you didn't exist yet. It denies you all substance and droningly echoes that there was no proof of your presence on Earth barely an hour ago. As for me, I remember finding in the rag I was wringing above the bucket a ball of hair belonging to our dog Prince, dead for three years. Wiping up dust in a damp rag is another entirely valid way of ridding yourself of it. When you've drawn up the full inventory of what you've agreed to do without, all that's left is cleaning up and resuming life in a place sanitized—for a time—of yourself, and where you can once again walk barefoot and lay on a stone or wood floor without fear of crushing even the smallest grain of rice or encountering the tip of a needle.

Since neither ants nor mice nor birds are allowed in the house, we must sweep up the crumbs that have fallen from the table. Every meal ends up there, on the ground—which is to say on the floor. We find salt, bread, sugar, pasta, flour under the table and with these esteemed leftovers it's possible to make a substantial cake. We just need to find the binding agent that would bestow a divine cohesion upon everything. Let's say the cement exists, that it is known and time-tested. Let's say egg is the binder in question. I stick together each grain of rice to which I add each crumb of bread. I dredge noodles with salt and pepper and roll them in flour. Hair and eyelashes give it structure, like cow's hair in ancient mortar. Who wants some? Instead, I sweep up these leftovers that have become unusable. These little particles that our mouths couldn't swallow, that our fingers couldn't hold—now no one can enjoy them. Whatever it be, I remain custodian of this wasted portion, which I hasten to clear away into the trash or toss out the window for the birds, mice and ants for whom I am neither begetter nor provider—just a distant relative.

Scrubbing a wood floor isn't as enjoyable as rinsing off a tiled floor checkered with white and black slabs. Wood floors absorb much of the water that you splash on them.

19

They protest by emitting the strong odor of wet wood. When you begin to wash an old oak floor—a floor blackened with wax and smoke—it must be seen through to the end and cleaned until it shines. A thousand pails of water wouldn't be enough. You must choose to harden the filth of the floorboards in an oily, dense beeswax or, by leaving it entirely bare, bleach it with consecutive baths. You thus obtain, after many moons, boards the color of driftwood. But only vacuum when they are dry. The smell of wet wood is the smell of slums, sunken ships and houses in ruin. The nose has a good memory for desolation.

But flooding is how I wash the stone tiles in the corridor. We can't have visitors be frightened when they first step into the house. Soaked, the black stone (that we call blue) is perfect, deep and opaque. As it dries it pales, deciding to conceal its dark heart under a film of salt.

Above all, let no one catch me with a rag in hand and galoshes on my feet.

When you sweep and wash, you soil yourself. Then you can only dream of returning your clothes to a state that's clean, elegant—like new.

Nothing extraordinary will happen. The extraordinary won't take place. Or else it's already in progress, gradually blossoming or withering, and dissolved into daily life like a leaf among foliage. Noticing it is like deciding to distinguish this leaf among all others, to specify its form—its position on the branch, its serrated edge, its changing color—and to follow its metamorphosis day after day until it falls to the ground and is transformed into humus or ash. So, once and for all, we will have seen the extraordinary fall and meld into communal earth and there lose all its fundamental characteristics, its appearance, its reason for being.

To write in winter I need two loads of wood a day so that the fire in the stove never dies. I need to be warm to write. To write, I need to know that all the other people in the house are warm. And even if I don't write a single line, I burn two loads of logs a day. At what point am I starting to waste this precious wood? How much must I want to write to merit a fire in my study? After what number of lines scribbled on the page can I deem the fire isn't burning in vain? Should the quality of these lines be taken into account when calculating gains and losses? I don't like lighting a fire for nothing, and yet I have to light it to see if I'm in any position to write, even if only one line. When I write, I don't hear the fire; I don't feel it either, so much so that I sometimes let it go out. But when I can't write, I distinctly hear the stove devouring the logs one after another, as quickly as I load them, and I'm so warm that I've got to take off several layers of clothing. When, after laboriously writing nothing, I return to our bedroom, the shift from sauna to icebox gives me the wretched sensation of having lost three times over: my time, our wood and my elbow grease. I'll only have been warm, even too warm, and for nothing. It's during these evenings of dreadful heat that I catch all my colds. In these moments I feel like a locomotive launched full speed downhill; I foresee my imminent dissolution. This fire must serve—I often say to myself—it must serve, on pain of drying out my innards.

Ironing shirts, pants and dresses sometimes takes a whole day in a warm mist, with steam and the quest for a remarkable and satisfying perfection. When I iron, seldom though I do, I iron as I have seen it done—in a grand silence where I am the lone workman. I'm accomplishing a great feat for I'm bringing life to corpses and I'm smoothing out sheets of papyrus to display stunning cosmogonies for all to see. I lay the intrepid iron shield flat upon the scorching field. I emblazon coats of arms. In truth, I emblazon every time I iron. I can't stop myself. I am slow by nature and am forced to eradicate the faces that I find in every wrinkle. This work consists of erasing lines and figures. It's about conjuring the human silhouette in its grace and fragility from the clutter. The grotesque silhouette.

I make creases in clothes disappear like I'd polish gold leaf. I unfold the sea and the surface of a lake furrowed by wind. I can only progress extremely slowly for at any moment I run the risk of watermarking baleful scenes on our finest flags—such scenes as would demand a new washing to expunge. The wind and my fiancée inhabit the large dress that I lay out. The wind and Louise enter the little dress and the air and Marin dwell together in the short pants because in the air our clothes unfurl like wreathes of smoke.

I've just got to tidy a jumble of colors that are gearing up to return to the savagery of the hordes, hills and skies.

An imposing silence ensues from this activity and little by little overtakes the room we've chosen, once and for all, to finish this job.

Despite having tackled so much, the pile of laundry never shrinks. Seems like it's alive—fermenting and rising. Finally, when everything's finished and the heat has dispersed and along with it the silence, I have to put away the laundry, nimbly and with care, in precise compartments—in other words, in their place, in wardrobes jampacked with domestic order.

Facing the heaps of rumpled rags all crammed into wardrobes, we often realize the utter uselessness of the task we seek to foist on ourselves. That's just too bad! We push the pile back into a corner. But it's only been put off until later. It's here that we can set aside a moment to begin sorting what can be worn tomorrow and what's no longer in style, and what needs mending. There are holes where the bordering fabric is but a ghost. To each his role, to each his task.

Sewing buttons back on a coat or shirt is thoroughly pleasant. Whatever's buttoned should always know to what its integrity is tied. The essential material for this work is very light and may be held in the palm of your hand; if not for the danger that the sharp and obstinate needle represents to the tender little palm residing between the four allied fingers. It's the stuff of magic. Disparate and faintly contradictory qualities give it a ludic nature. It's quite precious—most of the time misplaced and scattered—and all the elements that comprise it, its constituents, are both common and cheap. This entails nothing thrice: a spool of black, white or blue thread; the thimble (sometimes in the shape of a cup); and, of course, the aforementioned needle. Everything seems simple and self evident, but the missing buttons must first be found. In principle, not just any buttons can be used—only the right ones, the original buttons. For someone who can never remember where he keeps loose change and whatnot, this search proves hopelessly difficult. But the tailor doesn't get upset. He thinks things over. Without moving, he speculates, opening numerous drawers in his mind. He knows that the buttons are tacked according to style and size to rectangles of cardstock and that these cards are filed away in an old candy box. He becomes beside himself, but he can't remember where this box can be found, for the good reason that he neglected to fix in his memory the form and color of that little chest with the cover that doesn't screw off, but is popped off by pressing on its center. He can hear its characteristic noise. He fumes.

He searches for the missing buttons as he would search for every tooth in his mouth, scattered indiscriminately in time and in space.

The moment the buttons fell must be remembered at all costs. Identifying these exact instants will indicate, with perfect clarity, the places where they reside. Most of the time, the buttons have found a secure place within a very confined perimeter of where they fell: at the edge of the fireplace, in a saucer or in an unused ashtray. They've often christened a new container, infinitely multiplying the indispensible reliquaries and forever disassembling our scattered skeleton—the nails and the screws of our coffins (tomorrow is not yesterday) and the seeds in our capitula.

From time to time, the would-be tailor must surrender. This means he already knows where to find the type of genie and organizer who can answer all his questions.

Against the extreme aggressiveness of the needle the thimble was designed to be a kind of stolid ring.

Usually, the would-be tailor refuses to dip the flesh of any one of his fingers into this tiny silver chalice. First of all, he's not afraid of the kind of jab he's opening himself to and what's more, being a born klutz, he could only make poor use of the armor offered to him. Fewer factors, fewer errors is his lifelong motto.

It just so happens that buttons can be lost forever. A quick trip to the haberdasher in order to pick out a new set of buttons, which the would-be tailor likes to be entirely smooth and slightly convex like lentils. A new, complete collection of buttons doesn't make a new garment, much less a new man. However, barely visible and varied marks may bring to this half-certainty the idea that new buttons might lead to an (imperceptible) revitalization of gestures and general attitude.

It just so happens that a spool of thread is almost swapped for one in a similar color—say, black for a navy blue garment or white for a gray garment. It won't upset the order of the universe.

At home, it's rare to be unable to get your hands on a needle. The question of the needle isn't frequently asked in a house where someone takes it upon himself to put even the smallest speck in order. There's always a needle jabbed in a rectangle of black or white cardboard, or into the body of a spool, perceptible at the end of luminous strings, like a comet. And so we learn that certain celestial bodies have a life much nearer our own than we might think, and with a certain domestic quality.

Sometimes, we yank out the needle by following the white thread, weighing the needle's mass in steel, made of an amalgam of stuff—soft, light and indefinable.

Here we find the eye's enigma—there is always something in the way of the thread passing through the needle's eye. I swear to you that there's actually some sort of membrane covering it up. Invisible, but entirely existent. Only a magic incantation will dispel it. It might seem that it's the air itself compressed to the extreme into that small passageway that forms the barrier.

A single guiding principle: never try to sew even one button on a garment you, yourself, are wearing or else you might not only sew yourself to it like inside a pouch, but also risk sewing new misfortune into the lining.

On the coat spread out on your knees, as you sit by the window, all the buttons can now be carefully resewn, like they were once, so well that you wonder why they always end up falling off sooner or later. Who gives the signal for revolt, button or thread? It's true that no bond can resist time.

In the same way that elaborate swerves and snags stand in the way of venturing straight ahead, there are dozens of needle eyes that make it so that time, in a single block, dives in and expands in a passage so narrow that it seems to disappear entirely without leaving a trace.

Suddenly, obsessed with black thread, you find it everywhere—on the floor and even cooked into pancakes. And my mother would've never been my mother if a bit of black thread hadn't adorned the corner of her lips.

Tidying the children's toys, clothes and various objects scattered by tantrums confers an almost divine status upon she who knows each thing's rightful place. In the emptiness surrounding us, we must construct a full line of shelves in the form of ladders. We must negotiate a multitude of drawers in densest darkness. We must at the very least place objects and clothes out of reach of dust, fly droppings, pigeon shit and the ever-present light. We must invent storing places for our cherished goods and perishables. No house can function in ignorance of the state of these reserves. So sheltered from the light of day, our goods regardless aren't so shielded from the abuses of time. Certain clothes fall into fashion's oblivion, losing their charm and reason for wearing them and others acquire an overrated worth. Contact must be maintained constantly—airing and taking stock of these reliquaries and getting rid of objects whose smell testifies to a too potent indifference. There isn't only one way to tidy, but thousands—each necessary for structuring and mapping out the existence of the house, which is (well before it appears to be a system of doors, windows and walls) a whole system of alveoli. The simplicity of domestic life flows from the vast complexity of these alveoli. Just as you need a place for soap, you need a place for books. A place for sleeping and a place for sitting. A place for thumbtacks and a place for salt. A place for perfume and a place for stench. She who knows the place of each thing is capable of measuring the household's degree of destitution or richness. Before stocking the reserves, you first need money to buy spacious cabinets. Before possessing treasures, you need to possess the furnishings to house them. The easiest objects to put away, those that straightaway have their place, are the kids' toys. All the little characters go straight to their little houses, the cubes in their carts, the tools and materials in their trucks.

When they've been retired from use, it's because they're no longer indispensible or because it proves necessary to restore our interest in them, to plunge them for a short time in a beneficent bath of forgetfulness where their countenance acquires carats and carats of enchantment. Still these abductions must take place at the opportune moment. You must, above all, foresee the seasons of resurrection, taking into account the brevity of all things.

He who whistles in the house is known for throwing money out the window. But what does it matter if it's out the window or into some other chasm? Would money still be lacking? Yes, but much in the same way as matches would be at the moment when they seem indispensible, or a sewing needle, or a nail when the hammer's already in hand and the wall marked by a pencil with a cross. In this house, the lack of money is unwelcome as a migraine, a visceral cramp, a sour stomach or a nervous breakdown. Money will never be a remedy against insomnia, the speed or the slowness of time and even less against the anxiety of early morning or evening. Because, little by little, everyone here measured its efficacy. Be that as it may, when it's lacking, the dirtiness of the walls jumps out at you, the acid creeps up the esophagus, the migraine takes an endemic turn and the dust, at once perceptible to all five senses at once, acquires a savage tenacity. Sometimes the lack of money is like a door latch and when you notice its disappearance, you realize all the things that are deficient: a certain molar, a roomier cabinet, a change of scarf (your only scarf always smells of tobacco). Five thousand tulip bulbs would barely suffice to dress up the edges of the parti-wall. In that moment, the (always unwelcome) rain is more humid, the earth is more acidic, and the wind whistles through window cracks. I am not responsible for the lack of money. It's not I who invented that lack. So why should I make up for it? I breathe, I walk, I give kisses and I receive them. I have good shoes, and when I come back from a walk, a pair of slippers waits for me on the second step of the stairs. What is my viaticum? Should I gather my weight in white beans? What is my worth in this world? How much must my children be paid by the virus that will devour my liver or the owner of the tree whose pear will have shattered my skull? After all, coins are only bits of disfigured happiness from the dismembered body of an ancient dragon who belongs to us all.

Here are my slippers. If you come into my house, you might very well see them. I wouldn't put them on, of course, under your nose, but there's a good chance your eyes will fall upon them under a chair or sticking out from beneath a wardrobe. They're neither so ugly nor so shameful that I need to conceal them from visitors' view at all costs. Rather, out of respect for you, I just wouldn't have them on. You might well see many other things that belong to the house, and you may even smell the smells of the house where I live. It's not meant to offend you. What you needn't see has been carefully tidied away. Yet there still may be particular details that may shock you. We've scattered here, a bit all about, the traces of our life and it's not in our power to efface them. By searching a bit, you could find eyelashes on the table and hairs on the backs of chairs—a feeble testament to our private life. In this house, we live relentlessly, filling eternity with our detritus. And those scraps we've shed rot in this depository that we've created to our liking, that we've never stopped christening. Invisible rats live there and eat their fill on countless gulls lighter than air. And you—visitor, companion, life-long friend—I am that which is concealed to you, a sensation between vague nausea and indistinct desire, inevitable rejection. When I visit others' homes, I look for their slippers, for hairs between a comb's teeth or amongst the bristles of their brushes. In books loaned to me, it's the snot or the shred of dead skin magnetically stuck between pages.

Why aren't there more wardrobes? Why is there never enough room to put away our clothes? Contrary to what you might believe, too many clothes is not a sign of wealth. Because, in your collection, you've kept items you haven't worn for ages but are nevertheless wearable. If wardrobes overflow, it's not because they're jammed with fine garments or precious textiles, but because they're too small and poorly equipped to accommodate the castoffs of fifteen years of life that you can't bear to throw out. What's overflowing from the wardrobe is the inescapable surplus. Only wealth and spacious linen chests allow for such an unerring sobriety, such absolute austerity. Since the advent of time, wardrobes, dressers and chests have always been overloaded with this assemblage, odiferous and worn threadbare, and it won't stop anytime soon. The whole caboodle fortifies against adversity, keeping us warm under layers of mothballs. Would that ancient wool, one fiber stretched over another, shield us from misfortunes! It's only when the stench of mothballs disappears that the smell of soup and stewed apples can begin to waft through the house.

And now, what four or five mouths will eat needs to be prepared and cooked. It's not enough to select the ingredients—you need to put them in a pot and follow the recipe step by step. During cooking, the windows are open and all the sounds from outdoors drift into the kitchen and the smell escapes into the garden where it delivers fragrant messages. From the garden, a multitude of echoes swells. The wind whistles across the burner, slowing the cooking. Butterflies and wasps come by. The flies will arrive later for the spoils. The vegetables remain enslaved to the humus and bonds renew regardless whether a male or female cook presumes to rule over the world, pulling all the strings, ready to tear or cut. The universe will cook in the pot, but the principal puzzle is to get it in there all together and to hold it prisoner long enough to extract its essence. It tries to free itself from the trap, escaping over and over, from top and bottom, through cover and base. Soon it will infiltrate the house from foyer to third floor bedrooms. Quick to boil over, it proves pervasive everywhere except where it's been locked up, cut to pieces, crumbled and delicately chopped. Every day the monster with a hundred-thousand heads and two-hundred-thousand arms, employing a hundred-thousand ways to evade being cooked, cooks in the pot. So why try to fit it all in one soup? So that, at the end of the line, at least one particle of immensity remains. So why in such a small pot? So that it'll suit our needs. And why persevere in wanting to cook it all? To finally succeed.

So now this universe simmers, reduced to more scalable proportions. And now it gets transformed into tiny, tasty morsels, and now it's divided into four or five portions and is swallowed right away. And then infinity, ceaselessly growing and reconstituting its breadth, passes through the eye of the needle, the stranglepoint of our throats, piercing us with joy and sundry agonies. It's at this exact moment when the entire universe toils in the narrow circuits of our bodies that we run the day's greatest risk. The danger of suffocating and bursting are so great that each of us holds our breaths, yawns to allay suspicion and emits a self-satisfied burp. In much the same way as we've always kept

the fire, we retain in our guts the seeds of our decomposition, our forthcoming transformation. The raw ham
attracts wasps. Who gave me life is a question that nags
at the individual in the throes of digestion.

Why was I born is a question best asked after meals—specifically, between two meals, in that uncertain interval as one
goes about lighting tobacco and discharging its smoke from
the nostrils. Born from flesh and on flesh fed, producing
only flesh, putrid and poignant, yet a connoisseur of fire,
casting the blue of smoke against the blue of sky, like cobras,
knotted ropes disappearing into clouds, friendly genies of
boundless power. The smoker momentarily resents flesh
because by smoking he's become a spirit unfolding into the
upper strata of the atmosphere, in the so-called heights, in
the ether. He feels the need to disinfect this blasted moldy
cave where he dwells. So he forms wreaths of flowers, of
bindweed, fleeting garlands and, if near the sea at the end
of the meal, he turns his worried face and mouth filled with
bitterness towards absolute bitterness, and pine pitch intoxi-
cates him. Sometimes he encounters an ineffable flesh so soft

it makes him lose his footing. And from a mixture of flesh, he makes a divine potion that is at once phlegm, whey and cum, perfume and laughter. At times he folds himself upon himself and, in a familiar exchange, makes do with whatever he can bestow himself. The tobacco went out quite some time ago, dissipated and still no response has been provided to the original question, proving that the query was only ever meant as a diversion, a simple after-lunch pastime.

Let there be stew! I consecrate Friday to red cabbage that I slice in half then into quarters after washing it. White light is present in red that blues. I slice my thoughts into strips, filled with azure-glutted sky. I carried this head of cabbage under my arm without weighing the light it contained. I destroy its organization. I cleave a rock and strip the minerals from it that heat will melt. Let there be stew, garnished with lard and sausage smoke like an ancient sun forever unyielding. No one can know the full list of ingredients flavoring this concoction—not even he who's charged with its concocting, the so-called game master. The finished stew is the result of a combination of circumstances. All we can say is that disparate forces acting according to their own devices have contributed to the texture of the dish. Now that's what we can say, all while digging up an infernal hunk of sausage with a wooden spoon, all swollen and bursting in the serene, boiling magma. Nothing escapes the incredible odor of cooking cabbage, its arrogant aroma that would be gruesome were it not (as if to excuse itself) warm, mildly soured by apples, primal and barely just preserved by a secret alliance with all other domestic perfumes. The domestic cook is a conjugal cook. He deserves no praise for accomplishing the task he's obliged to complete. The domestic cook doesn't have to show off. Let him bring braised quail or bangers and mash to the table—the reception will be the same. He is but the simple, temporarily culinary transcriber of the house's spirit. The sole thing asked of him is the prompt delivery, at the right time, of the script. To each his role. Chef, contractor of tasks, high or low.

Some days, when the odor of cabbage has dispersed, when the spirit of oranges on the platter has calmed, an overpowering odor resurfaces and rises to garden level. It's like the smell of a turtle or poorly scrubbed latrines. It's sometimes so strong, so sharp that you ask yourself what's decomposing and where. A monstrosity takes form in the darkness, in the dampness, in the soot and saltpeter. It's so strong, so sharp you ask yourself that very moment if it hasn't been reigning for all eternity and if it isn't rather this odor that, from time to time, surrenders before the tenacity of this squalid creature and if you mightn't forever wear the sign, the trace of it, and if, no matter where you go, you'll peddle this fearful family odor that makes us known and infamous throughout town, that precedes us everywhere. What do I smell like? What's my basic odor? Are we already so soaked in the dampness of cellars, I and all who dwell in this house, already so marked by the sign of the mold from which the cascades and cascades of blue wisteria will never absolve us? How are we not already shapeless and slimy from so much infamy? On the spalling brick, on the rotting wood, on the balmy gloom of the depths fall cascades and cascades of blue clusters, of this blue on the edge of disappearance, of oblivion, this crimsoning blue, this apoplectic blue. In the world, the monstrous mold encounters the monstrous wisteria that is constantly regenerated from its frailty, and, together, they create the

40

lavish and mortal paradise of summer. And in the stair-
well where spirits convene, the smell of rotting meets the
aroma of soup.

Each day the scene repeats itself. I sit facing Louise. Louise sits to the right of Carine. Carine sits facing Marin.
Marin sits to the right of Louise. Spoons are lifted. Forks,
set. On the ceiling, there is a congregation of flies, the
same ones as a hundred years ago. As for us, we are a
congregation of ogres and ogresses, assembled for the
feast. And we've decided to face each other, in a square,
so even the tiniest flavor does not escape us, so as to
share in the thrill and keep vigil over a fair distribution.
Thus assembled, we are ready to gobble a mountain of
potatoes, loads of lamb, a cow, even an elephant. Animals
fear us. But eyes are always bigger than bellies. They have
a good sense of excess. As for us, we content ourselves
with little, but have a yen to devour the world. We live in a
gingerbread house. We drink birch sap from glasses made
of sugar and when grief torments us, drops of brine fall
from our eyes. We need light to eat—sun, honey or incan-

descent light. Marin's foot is balanced on his mother's knee since the height of the table allows it. And Louise looks at me in the whites of my eyes.

A family always gathers around a table. It's the family of bread. It's the family of salt and pepper. It's the family of slices of cucumber and salami. It's a family that ripens bananas and transforms wine to vinegar. It welcomes a fish with much consideration, then chops it into bits. It hunts for fish bones in the white of the dish. A family of four or five mouths devours a whole chicken in just a few mouthfuls. It gives off the aroma of vegetable soup. The family is most delicate when exuding this sweet scent, yet also most whole. Danger is most imminent when the soft fragrance of a baking cheese tart spreads through the household. Ensconced in its bliss, the family drops its essential vigilance and latent peril takes the form of a train hurtling down the station's access ramp, of a voice on the radio, of a dirigible filled with combustible gas, of total eclipse. But, although made of such flimsy material, this bliss is the most stable element in family life, ceaselessly fabricated, easy to reproduce and reproducing itself ipso facto like carbon dioxide. Asking why this bliss doesn't last is another way of asking why we do. But the family persists, feeding on nothing, like how people fed on ants and roaches throughout the Stone, Bronze and Iron ages. A family isn't necessarily peaceful. A family can be thoroughly anxious and tormented, keeping an eye out for cracks, smoke, strange smells. They're as sensitive to the hatching of moth eggs as to the faint flickering of the lights. These upheavals are scrutinized before being accepted. Bliss may be defined as a space empty of venom or gruesome junk. It's set off from the days when all matter possessed a kind of harmony, as if it were fermented and immediately digestible whatever its form. A family moves about with its effects and its laments, and its specific odor. A family takes a boat one sirocco night and journeys to an island. From the hills, they'll take the time to watch the zephyrs' remnants across the surface of the sea.

If done precisely with the help of a small knife with a thin blade that some call a peeler, peeling apples amounts to a game of skill. You can watch the blade as it slides under translucent skin. And, in your hand, you see a sort of phylactery unfurl, detailing the full surface area of the fruit. This is a job that, if left only to me, would be eliminated evermore from the manuals of domestic life because an apple is a whole; the skin belongs to the flesh, the flesh is complete with the skin. Be that as it may, it's worth the trouble. No activity, apart from washing dishes, is as soothing. From the instant that children ask for their slices of apple to be bestowed to them without the peel, peeling becomes necessary and eminently interesting. Peeling becomes a way of being, a way of weighing the pros and cons, of conducting yourself in relation to objects, of searching under the skin for the illumination of flesh. Be there two, ten or twenty apples to peel, you must try hard to do it in the same manner—first lifting the thinnest possible sliver and then, with the tip of the knife, getting rid of bruised flesh and popping the seeds from their burrows.

Constant cleaning is crucial for everything that has sprouted, wilted, molded and rotted in the depths of pantries and refrigerators. Constant throwing out surplus is called for. We fill up buckets, we tie up bags and we transport them as far as possible from the kitchen—actually out of the house, out of the garden, right behind the gate. Could the dump begin just beyond that gate? Could it begin in the distance where I tossed my peels—that's to say less than a stone's throw from the threshold of the house? And when I'm old and bedridden, will the dump have caught up with me? Or will I be on top of it, barely able to recognize myself in the scraps in that reeking compost heap? I will be emptied of everything before doing myself in, thrusting my whole life into a future so near and irremediable that, at long last, I'll be able to confess to having joined it at birth. I'll be able to say: here I am dead, it had to happen—or even: here I am, dead. In the meantime, every day bins are filled and emptied and dumps go ignored by most everyone, except for the rats, gulls, magpies, starlings and, in some countries, bears. Part and parcel of the pleasure of eating is the worry of making what's left disappear in one way or another—diligently so. The cumbersome remnants of happiness have their rightful place by our side, and no distance, no fence, no depth can make us ignore and forget them. Each house should have a small (or large) private dump neighboring the rose garden. Manure has its place in the charming courtyard, just beneath the dining room windows. There are delicacies to banish, a sense of smell to be trained and an eye to be preserved from the veils of steam.

In the manner of birds who ruffle their feathers, we stretch ourselves across our skeletal frames as if on stilts, to show off. Once dead, without funeral pomp, folded onto our bones, we settle to the bottom of a bag.

Why do trash bins reek is a way of asking why do trash bins exist.

The stench can't be dissipated. Everyone gets it like they were born for it. The smell of vomit on some of the dishrags is just mind-boggling, at once sour and sweet. An organism sometimes goes haywire, and consequently flowers no longer smell of rose or lily-of-the-valley. Something ebbs toward the light. Does an ever-expanding universe dream of pure air and a yellow moon with holes in it? Oh, how I hate to stink! There are days when a horrid odor exudes from ourselves, like smoke and soot from a butcher's oven.

Water boils and steam glazes the windowpanes. Another world is brewing and growing in size. Boiling water has its own smell, a smell you perceive right away. All the qualities favorable to its perception—heat, lightness and humidity—are contained in it. It takes on a perfect form, volatile and warm. We breathe in its spirit, which travels through us. In the kitchen where the kettle boils, a long-standing phenomenon repeats itself for which I am one of the final witnesses, the one from this very day. I am witness to boiling and evaporation; the humidity touches

47

and moves me. I no longer see trees. I no longer see clouds and I no longer see roofs. I live in a fragile tent that I pretend is a women's skirt, a slightly pinkish skirt—it's the setting sun. I have no money. I'm congested and the steam soothes me. I live in another world, one of relative opacity, of actual water, of the laundry room, of translucent sheets, of limbo, of fog and of dawn. I am alive, anxious and annoyed. Suddenly our poverty appears to me in all its breadth, but it only lasts until the acid in my stomach reabsorbs and each time it dies down without resolving. I toss florets of broccoli into the boiling water and in doing so I keep them from rotting.

Having once been in a stomach, in that stomach, brings a vitality back to me that I'm tempted to believe is eternal.

On this very day, this exemplary day, in no time at all, the splendor of a half salmon, accompanied by florets of broccoli and a modest portion of new potatoes, was acheived. It took fire. It took water. And it took light, in all its simplicity. Sometimes what we eat possesses the rough and rugged qualities of earth, other times airlike traits. It so happens that various qualities come together in thirty-six ways and among these numerous combinations there's one that is exceptional—the rebirth of a recipe from antiquity. This miracle takes place thus—we feast on leaves from the trees and on mushrooms from the ground. It so happens sometimes that we eat truffles along with pig's snout and snails from the thrush's anvil. But these coincidences are rare and we recognize these moments thanks to a sort of break in the weather, an astonishingly sunny spell. We then give ourselves over to food in the same manner as we bathe in the sea, with steady breath, safe from any sudden seizure, reaping the benefits in snippets, sighs and quick glances, as if in the middle of making love where the amplexus welds us to the skin of another, to its color, its tact, its palpitations. Now to soak garlic bread in soup or tomato juice, mushy from the salt, and savor heaven in each mouthful, in the flavor of stone, iron and spelt. All of a sudden, the mix of yeasts and sediments that we bring to our mouths meets those our bowels contain, and they liquify. We no longer know what it is we're eating. We no longer know if we're eating or if we're eaten. At the pinnacle of happiness, we let air issue from our lips, like children organizing a tea party, mute and dry. And, suddenly, it could be ourselves we're devouring, our seasoned and appetizing selves. From a few yards under the table, the basement, a bed we make, expands.

You must always renovate your residence beginning with the basement.

Coal is black, heavy, powdery and rank. But it glistens, even in the half-light of the cellar. When I go down, I discern it piled against the wall, remarking on its volume and dampness. It won't come up on its own from the place it was thrown in anticipation of a hard winter. You need to ferret it out. You need to go down in the cellar that has become the repository for several generations of neglect—dirty, full of bottles, of blackness, smoky, damp, fertile and uninhabited. Going down to the cellar you reach the bottom of the house, the vast self-evident, ancestral misery; vast because we could never measure its extent, because we always postpone the task of combing through it until the next day; self-evident because it's immediately perceptible, rank, damp and smoky; and ancestral because as far back as we can remember it's always the same image that forms over and over, decaying, even poisoning the sight of the sky. Why have beautiful, light, spacious rooms on the second floor if the cellar remains a cloaca and quagmire? It's true that immaculate white eggs come from cloacae and mauve foxglove from quagmires. A cellar should be a place of preference, much like a living room or bathroom—a kind of dewy, cool, slightly chalky and welcoming household temple; and never a place where you throw objects that you no longer want to see and that very quickly become squalid and even ignominious things. A cordial line of contact should be upheld with what is called (according to the laws of gravity) the ups and the downs. Or else we run the risk of losing our feet in the mire, of having our head interred in dust and retracting into our shoulders.

Two stove-fulls per day empty the cellar of its reserve of coal. It's a damp and foggy winter, and the smell of rotten eggs stagnates beneath the roof of the house. Nothing rises. Nothing escapes. We live on a pile of coal and in a cloud of smoke. We are sooty and smoky, and we sense ourselves collapsing at breakneck speed. During the day, we search for the sun and at night, the moon. We lack light far more often than heat. We consume ourselves at the same rate as the coal. We find ourselves at the end of an impasse, in the cul-de-sac of the world, incapable of moving and hoping for the miracle of snow, the only thing in a position to metamorphose our life. We've become so unconcerned with the quality of light that a candle flame burnishes our eyes and a tiny strand of the moon renders us our shadow. At such a time it's necessary to leave the house and dissolve in the fog, walk and use your body and the breath that animates it like a lifeboat. We have to remind ourselves over and over, sometimes violently, that we are animated, inhabited by air and that we must move and realize our longings in the open air. We have to face the rough winter, walk in obscurity and dissolve in dampness. And thus, little by little, we leave our despondency for we cannot curse the element of which we're part and parcel. We cannot scorn the cankers that gnaw at us.

Sometimes you have to take extreme measures against the mold in the walls. Let the walls collapse. Who cares? But what if it's emitting an unbreathable and deadly dust, the exact opposite of golden rain and celestial manna! The walls can't withstand the emptiness they contain. Nothing gnaws so quickly as emptiness. The walls were established to partition the emptiness of space, to trap it, and no function is more tenuous than enclosing space itself, this age-old time, this fossil that's survived every cataclysm, singular or ongoing. So under the pressure of this great reptile they crumble, and they start crumbling from the moment they're built, and the materials start crumbling from the moment they're chosen, hewn or fired, for they are composed of permanently crumbling matter. With fragments and powder, we can only make agglomerates of fragments and powder. We find shards of fool's gold in the thickest ramparts and cow hairs in posh parlor walls. And sea salt and lichen break down the structure of the tiles and bricks fired at the highest temperatures. We fill in, we disinfect, we repaint and we preserve a new eternity. That's all we can do.

When an old pear tree dies, you have two options. Either you cut it down to soil level, or you can use its boughs and trunk as supports for a rose bush, wisteria or clematis. In that way its doleful silhouette remains and the regular arrival of flowers decorates it like a constellation of wishes. But it's possible that no wishes come true because the pear tree resists any and all mercy or because no plant can adapt to the base of a dead tree. We wanted, we dreamt, but year after year nothing we'd hoped for succeeded. So, we can cut it down to ground level or be content with its naked silhouette and scaly bark. Every intervention in the countryside has absolutely uncertain results, where even the smallest success always seems a miracle. Sometime, over the years, some plant probed the ground in search of water and pockets of nutrients. It's stunted, it searches, and then, abruptly, takes root and sends out shoots.

We enter the garden to bear witness to wonders and to lament destruction. The garden remains a laboratory and a work zone in perpetual development. And the strength of development is that all phenomena participate in it: the disintegration of the dead pear tree, the growth of suckers, the low wall caving in, the suffocation of the lawn beneath a proliferation of moss. But isn't moss as good as fine grass when barefoot?

A garden occasionally assumes the spirit of its gardener, all the while constantly eluding his morality. He takes a hands-off approach and flees from it like mint flees the box you planted it in and escapes. Kinships appear between the most dissimilar species. We are tempted to put stinging nettles into our mouths. And suddenly the green becomes an ardent blue or a glistening black.

I don't want to do anything on Monday afternoon, and so I arrange my isolation. I sit in the fragile caned chaise-lounge that I've oriented in the right direction. This will be an afternoon full of flies. There are nine of them around the light fixture. I'm hoping to be visited by a wasp, handsome as a sugared cake, always bringing company. And, little by little, as my arm (that I can't be bothered to hold up) falls from the armrest and as a host of creatures (with an incomparable accuracy and dexterity) live their immediate lives accompanied by nervous, rhapsodic buzzing, and having placed my measuring equipment—cups and spoons and sticks and tapes—far out of reach, I cease to exist on the inside, and my existence carries on in my extremities. My fingernails grow, my hair lengthens and my eyelashes fall—all without a sound and beyond my control, as if to the subtle rhythm of some well-hidden metronome. I don't want to do anything, but my lips can't stop themselves from forming maxims. It's then that the door, behind which I was hidden, opens and a golden silhouette with a round head appears, so close I could recognize it just by touch.

Where do all the clothes I wear come from? To cover my shoulders, my fiancée bought a linen shirt. To cover my worn out knees, my fiancée chose a pair of black twill pants, but my knees revealed themselves on the fabric soon enough, graying it with dead skin. So Louise wouldn't disappear entirely in stark light, Carine chose to dress her in a little red frock that trembles like a maple leaf in the gold and silver of the day. In his big trousers, Louise's older bother becomes a desert pomegranate tree. Overripe fruits rain down dyes. It's rose jam, flavored with petals; it's quince jelly on white bibs. All of the quilts have taken a pink shade and the sky has soaked our bed sheets with a pee that turns violet. She who dresses us chooses our go-to color. Louise will be violet every time that it proves necessary and Marin, gray at the right moment, like slate or a wood pigeon, which is to say, mysteriously mauve and hiding the satin lining on the back of his vest like a talisman of priceless purity. As for me, I will be black as tobacco or steel and Thalo blue like some Eastern Orthodox church roof, without ever deciding for myself. There will be lipstick on the hand towels and the dishrags will be stained with currant juice. The fences are all openwork—yards communicate and the neighbor's cherries and their fuchsia sometimes bleed onto our laundry and on our walls. It's from our old-fashioned rags that I choose my painting attire.

Once every hundred years the walls have to be repainted, the steel stripped back to white and the lead to light. And you apply the whitewash in successive layers until you've erased the shadows that have spread over time, nudging the house into chaos along the pitch of the road, opening large gaps in the walls that once were protecting us from the outer world. It proves necessary to block the holes before the whole town tries to slip a hand or a foot inside. For this, you don't use tar as with sea-fearing vessels, but a substantial and liquid white light. And we've only this curtain of whiteness at our disposal to fight off the assaults of the air and its fossilizing forces. But you mustn't think that by having accomplished this task you've eliminated all the shadows that have at their command—just as most creatures—at least one good way of being fruitful and multiplying, even if only in memory. The white light we use to cover leprosy and nodosity gives off the odor of curdled milk. It's an ancient milk, a star's milk, latex. Although not fully recommended by medical professionals, a latex bath is quite uplifting, a true degree of pleasure. To lay it down, you use a roller (once again this cursed purpose-built wheel) that disperses drops away from the direction it's moving. Like a lunatic, you spend your time rolling the ceiling, chasing black stars, craters, dead flies and you follow the traces of a impish fox leaving easy-to-detect trails with its sandy tail. You are so near the sky you could be right on top of it, but you can't see it. You try in vain to turn your neck at such unfamiliar angles that you're ready to somersault and adopt the candlestick pose. In this position, you see the world afresh, and you need a stool to get back onto your feet. At the base of the wall there always seems to be some enormous partition that makes you feel tiny and inconsequential. You say to yourself—brush in hand, conquered by discouragement, considering the stains of saltpeter and perhaps blood to be a fact of life—that, once the wallpaper's torn down, maybe you should've left the walls as they were. And so you renounce perfection.

The moment has come for me to sleep. I have to agree to separate myself from a series of things. Preoccupations no longer apply. Crumbs from the last meal have disappeared. Quietude has even reached the leaves of the ash tree that steadily quiver, all in the same plane, as if the whole tree forgot to consider the third dimension in which it had flourished until now, transforming itself for one night's time into a timeless skeleton. I clamber back up to the third floor, for we chose to sleep way up high, perched like crows, storks and vultures. If the attic were finished, we'd sleep up there so that we might be one with the sky, and in the dry heat the ghosts might evaporate. In each room we've placed a child. In one, a little girl and in the other, a boy. I go in to see them. Louise sleeps on her stomach and Marin on his back. Their mouths are open to let air and all its smells flow freely. If I put a bit of salt or sugar on their lips, they close right away. I need to make sure that no cat or bird is hiding under the bed and that the children are well bundled but not feverish. What is the right temperature for a carefree body? Only my fiancée whose backbone forms an inverted S in the whiteness of night knows. Have I accomplished all my tasks? Am I freed of all my burdens? Am I sufficiently naked and smooth to place my feet in the shared bed as if on the deck of a ship? Have I scrubbed all the decks, blown out the lights and shut off the gas so that it doesn't hiss that it's leaking? I grill myself while I stand. Did you bring up the chamber pot? Did you lock the doors? Did you put away the ladders? Is the wood stove filled for the night? Did you bring up the bedside glass and is it filled to the rim as it should be? Clean slate and rest fitting each fatigue.

On Wednesday, the moon, between black clouds, was the most luminous of moons. With my iron watering can, I sprinkled lunar months in rain water. I went from angelica to lilies and I had boundless generosity for the trees forming their first pears. Instead of going to bed, I stayed behind as if in a dream, in the night, imperfect and tranquil, specter or imposter wearing my sandals. I had soaked my feet and I could hear the water disappear into the earth like a comet with a scented tail. Filling the watering can with more water than it should hold, I traced pathways on the bricks and black shadows to the foot of the wall. With a pale hand, I made signs up to my lady in the window and to my children in their pajamas, watching them drift away as if in a boat. I continued dispersing water until the moon dissolved the town lights and lights from the highway ramp into a grand emulsion of cold milk that, illuminating me, brought me back to the present. I am the water bearer, the servant, and I work for the scarcely sick, for rose bushes, cherry trees, raspberry brambles. Believing that one day I was nearly plucked from the face of the Earth forever and that I must now content myself with the role of a toy Cartesian diver in the moonlight, and to renounce forever the role of a stump. Since, at this hour, I am the only being without roots, I have to bend at my knees and incline my spine. Since I am the only one with access to the water tank, I have to be the middle-man. I'm entirely bone and salt.

From the moment I move, the softness of my skin covers itself with bitterness. From the moment I rub it, my hide smells of burnt cow's horn. And from the moment I die, the iron in my blood returns to the rock and my lymph becomes white wine with a slightly golden tint.

I don't court death for I am far too indelicate. What's dead gets replaced.

Delicacy must be wrestled with what's on hand—with obstinacy, pruning shears, saw and spade. Delicacy is painstakingly tenacious and recurrent like mange. You can get rid of it only with a firm resolution, but you can never fully extirpate it. It continues to grow like fingernails and urges. It comes up like a grain and reseeds itself. Between rows of leeks, delicacy is like a dam of dodder, ground ivy and buttercups. Delicacy preserves the humus of sunburn. We are mistaken about the meaning of the abundance of flowers on an apple or peach tree and we delight in it, when in fact this unheard-of flowering is a sign of decline for the tree, of its asphyxiation. A waning tree continues to produce only flower buds, but no wood.

Radical decisions need to be made, namely to amputate, cut fifty-year-old branches to the trunk. Sometimes taking the tree down to almost ground level. And if the trunk is good, the tree will regrow. Each year of indecision slows this renaissance by an order of magnitude and diminishes its odds of succeeding. Sometimes delicacy takes us by surprise. Young nettles are so lovely and green like they'd been soaked in a bubbling spring, appearing on Earth at nearly the same time as snowdrops, that we object to pulling them up. So, at the speed of light they establish a new network of roots, doubling with the first of young, dense sheaves. We have a reluctant admiration for this initial luminous green. We decide to limit spontaneous vegetation at the moment it seems least vigorous, at the moment when the signs of Pierce's Disease underscore the edges of leaves. But it's clearly too late since new roots have already fed new branches, and seeds are already sprouting and the gestation is practically complete. We are like midwives frightened by blood, cries and sneezes, to whom nudity seems incongruous.

I move around at ground level and I am flat as a gecko, overcome by gravity. And I crawl around, searching for my tools.

One tool has always extended my arm. My hand has always been armed. My first knife was my sword and magic wand, a lever to lift mountains. I dream of a large universal spoon made of olive or boxwood that you can bite without fear of chipping a tooth, one you've always bitten, one that can dole out fried onion and garlic, that stirs soups, sauces, yogurt and jam. You might say the spoon sticks to my fingers and lips, so close to my tongue that it has a cradle there for resting the curve of its back. You might say all teaspoons are made of sugar, except when some rascal soaks them in sulfur. My mother gave me honey, syrup, marmalade and salt. Now I scoop them from pans and jars of my own volition. I measure the ingredients of my life and my tongue dreams of a spoon that never empties. Without the spoon, my mouth would've sealed itself and I'd have swallowed my tongue. The universe was composed from an intense suction whose pressure had to be released. It was formed at first by this suction and with a barely audible kissing sound. As for the knife, it was always in my hand. I never planted it in a heart, but I did bring down mountains with it! Nonetheless I use it parsimoniously, like someone who, each time he cuts something down, believes he's committed something irreparable. I always misplace my penknife and when I arrange the cutlery on the table, I always inadvertently set a fork on either side of the plate, for I could be Neptune's distant little cousin washed up on dry land. In olden days, when we were ogres and our mouths were huge and deep like baker's ovens, we used pitchforks to throw enormous chunks of meat therein. Invariably, we then had to adapt the instrument to our appetite.

The knife, too, is an instrument of measurement. It allows us to measure precisely the portion of the cake that is due everyone, the morning portion and the evening portion, the supplementary portion and the negligible portion, and the quantity of butter in which onions will brown. With this sort of instrument and with a bit of dexterity, a tiny praline, the last in the package, can be equitably divided between two, four, thirteen or thirty-six hungry mouths, and will please each one in a satisfactory way, according to the law of the division of a miniscule morsel of happiness among an infinite number of guests. The simplest miracles are born of this puzzle, since one turd of happiness easily suffices for each.

Was I born a mason without knowing it, for devoting such a love for the trowel that I use so little? Never has any tool seemed to me so suited to its function. Any clod who seizes it by the handle can just as soon mix sand and water into Portland cement (where the roses come in this famous verdigris foliage) or Roman *pozzolana*. There's always a hole somewhere to fill, or a crack to catch, or even a cavity to add to the structure of the world that burgeons and crumbles all at the same time. Neither a screwdriver nor fork can do anything against the crumbling of the world, whereas a hammer proves effective and persuasive, particularly the carpenter's hammer, with a head like a woodpecker, in the position to hasten its progress, and the trowel, to slow it.

Swiftly, at the speed of light, we name that which our fingers are unable to grasp.

What do you call the spoon that measures salt and carries it to a dying person's mouth? What do you call the knife used for skinning rabbits and goats? There should be a name for each square inch of the cutting board. There should be some vulgar and fitting designation for each toe and for each stage of a cadaver's decomposition, be it human being or donkey. The final stage, before the dissolution of the bones, when the wind causes odorless strips of leather to rustle, would be called extinction or sanctity or some shorter, cleaner word without any hint of histrionics.

But even the best laborer, mason, stonebreaker—he who ceaselessly practices his craft—never escapes nature's needs.

There's no getting around it—you have to pee. That little extra you've claimed as your own cannot be kept inside. The best is peeing outside against a wall, a tree trunk, on slightly dry bracken or even, with increased pleasure, into a stream of water rather than against a ceramic basin. But pissing from the height of a balcony, without fearing the splatter, merits special attention. A balcony lit by moonlight is needed and there's sometimes this marvelous sensation when the sound of the liquid falling on the ground is, as if by miracle—a timely benefit of the wind—imperceptible, flowing outside time and thwarting the laws of physics. And you find yourself within a hair's breadth of swan diving, of following the falling gold crossing infinity and in this way catching up with the tail of the comet, or some such. There is, in the judiciously managed urination of a man and a woman (when she decides to undertake it standing) with legs comfortably spread before a wall of ivy or at the edge of a balustrade, an exemplary posture with perfect equilibrium, as if taking atmospheric measurements with vital precision. A blissful, tantric pose is instinctively assumed, during which, if it were to last a century, the intimate fusion of every earthly element would be realized, or some such. If your feet get splattered, it just cools them off.

You know how to find it. A climbing rose bush excretes it and reveals its presence. The king goes there by foot, we used to say as children. Going to the toilet is far from being a chore. You may go there with the firm resolution of finding a treasure that occasionally boils down to a butterfly's wing therein. The toilet absolutely must be separated from the bath, if only by a burr elm door. One of the walls in the toilet must absolutely be pierced by a bright and easily opened window—an indeterminant style of window that is at once fan and sash. Wind, moonlight, cries from the gardens and the street sounds should reach this place that's kind of an improvised retreat at the heart of the daily chaos. During a heat wave, a shutter must let through a soft half-light. A pile of disposed terracotta tiles right beneath the skylight could, at certain times of day, throw a kiln red on the preferably whitewashed walls, casting a permanent and propitious dusk. No flowers, I beg you, and especially no wallpaper, made to look like tapestry. A bit of ink, some white sheets and a bit of chalk. The retreat is so short-lived that each second there is of the utmost importance And you prepare yourself, like before passing through a bottleneck in a cave. Then you relieve yourself of the world's weight. And suddenly you're so light and new, on the brink of levitation. What we do there preoccupies us. Only children and the elderly obsess over essential things. A beautiful, or funny, but dearly loved image is occasionally coveted there: it's the icon discovered in the sheepfold or the pious image in the pig-pen. There we tolerate burrowing bees' nests and woodlice, oh venerable crustaceans. But a merciless war will be fought against termites and shipworms. You're

69

terrified of seeing the throne sink into the floor, to disappear in the depths. Sometimes, with age, this fear of disappearing without a trace into the abyss makes us prefer to squat in open air, in a pine forest, on a hillside, in a Carmelite wood or better yet on a flat rock that forms a terrace. Then we relieve ourselves in the most orthodox position, placing our offering directly on the Earth's crust. Then, in lost moments like smoking after a meal or drifting off to sleep, it's fun to map out the best places to defecate, and to establish in this manner a sort of constellation thoroughly representative of the self.

You're always better wiped than you thought or you're always less wiped than you hoped. The fact of having a poor view of the situation because of the tricky sightline, makes us imagine the worst calamities or incredible perfections, according to the disposition of our spirit.

You never escape the patina of years.

Various powders patine the furniture, the hearth. No surface escapes them. There's a fine powder that falls from the dissipation of smoke and the downy dust that flies up from carpets and upholstery. You must never tackle the problem of dust on a sunny day; you might as well try to capture mites with a cinder sieve. You can never pretend to get all that dust, but simply contain its mass to within a reasonable area. When you decide to clear the dust with a mop or some sort of cloth, you must make a game of it, invest it with a healthy dose of skepticism and irony as if perpetuating an archaic rite by habit or compulsion, because there's no task more urgent on the horizon. For greater satisfaction, it's best to work in shadow and begin with the mantle, always loaded with slag. You might even dress up for the occasion, donning a hat—possibly a melon-shaped bowler or the winged stallion of a petase—and yellow gloves. Moreover, a tie decorated with pink frogs is entirely de rigueur. We go at the dust like we go to the theater, fresh, ready to be dumbfounded by smoke and mirrors. We attack this great eternal dragon, this saurian from before the flood with a popgun, an untarnished valor and a First Communion blazer buttoned like a steel breastplate. At any instant during the game you can take back your marbles and stuff the rag in the emblazoned pocket saying that the wind's in our favor, but unsolicited advice seems to warn us from committing the irreparable. So, respecting and resisting all reason, we continue catching phantoms with handkerchiefs. And the end catches us in the middle of a sentence. The wind's in our favor. It displaces the dunes and mountains, transports aromas and makes laundry flap.

The wind works in our favor. It dries our sheets and bears words and gestures. In this way, signs reach us from afar. In this way, everyone knows that you're cutting wood for more than a mile around, and whether you're splitting very hard logs with a massive axe. Everyone knows for more than a mile around that you're nailing the lid of a coffin or that you're screwing it down with squeaky screws. Everyone knows which path you're walking on. They hear your children. And the rooster can be heard practically from the other end of the neighborhood. The wind mixes us one with the other by carrying a rising, creeping smoke. Everyone knows what day the neighbor makes crêpes or doughnuts or roast chicken. The wind links us together and makes the bells chime and the boxwood branch scrape against the empty watering can. The wind fills us with silence and sound. The wind sweeps up dust and the wind brings back ancient daydreams to us. The wind fills us with worry and insomnia, but the wind also lulls us to sleep slowly or with an illusionist's dexterity and vivacity. The wind makes our skin start to peel, wears us out. We lean into the wind because the wind defends us from emptiness. It fills and supports us. The wind keeps delicacy at bay, though it ceaselessly expands like lichen. It tears petals from roses and shreds tree leaves. The wind's against us. It uproots apple trees and splinters the young olive trees. No cloud can resist it.

I will make crêpes every day of my life if for no other reason than to check to see if the recipe is right and if the taste is what I hoped it would be, like in olden days: seen, foreseen, heard in a story, breathed in dreams, formed from the world's simplicity. Eggs, flour, milk and salt—which is to say the entire world, the universe—go into one, like into a magic tower where everything disappears. We don't break eggs for nothing. Something good must come of them—an omelet, batter, mayonnaise or paint. We search for gold in the light, or silver, or copper, and we are very fond of phenomena. The batter that thickens during cooking and the fusion of all the elements are already lasting images, meaning at once diaphanous, dry or destined for desiccation, or as if foul, the gilded motifs and lace seeming at times like decorative motifs, other times like signs of mildew. The crêpes will be as supple as fine cloth. And from a single bowl of ingredients we can produce nearly a thousand that become terribly thin after the six-hundredth. So it goes, demonstrating to all who have any interest in it, whom the aroma has brought scurrying around, the true miracle of multiplication. And when everything goes down the drain, there are still crêpes, made from flour, milk, salt, fire, light, abundance and an appetite growing with each passing moment, like some sort of slow, polymorphic cogitation, finding on the gilt crust something for reflection, for begetting. We toss sugar on top, sparkling like fool's gold, or on a whim a bit of butter sweeter than gold and stars of salt. Then, stomach full, with your thumbnail, as if signing a register, you trace in the air or on the table, in a fit of pique or gratitude, something like *Nutrio et exstinguo*, in kitchen Latin or old Spanish, and we sleep in peace, or nearly. Fingernails and hair still growing.

When time allows, we push back against the re-emergence of urges with an exacting fervor, as if the working order of the universe depended on it. And, with this operation accomplished, we remain appeased by it, as if having satisfied a universal duty. While it would seem that few things satisfy us, this gesture is deeply soothing, as if it were part of an essential bath whose run of gestures was instinctively known and familiar to us, as if it were part of ancestral arrangements whose other movements were coitus, which is to say the immemorial rocking of a rowboat (at once obstinate and supple, regular and fantastical), heart beats, the use of a trowel, of a spoon and of the gravedigger's shovel; the cleaning of a long iron spade, the breeding of doves, the emptying of a chamber pot, the pruning of tree suckers and the keeping of bees. It's not beauty that's sought, nor perfection, but a balance of light, wind and how things stand. There is a moment when a yellow-colored stain on the tip of your nose flawlessly suits your general appearance. There are some gardens where grayed and porous collarbones and shoulder blades can cover the primrose beds, and others where menstrual blood can be sponged with cattails. In Italy, children are encouraged to be dirty and old people encouraged to be immaculately clean. There are rules and there are exceptions. My heart beating, nails clean with clear lunulae, I reveal myself to others with an astonishing composure.

This Thursday in May, I returned to my workroom where my window is open to ash boughs, hills, the sea and sky. As such, the ash returns to me or rather has never left, accompanying me in my ephemeral abode and enduring the same metamorphoses as me in the mild, sunny height of morning. Never will I forget that I am forever attached to a tree. Never will I forget that there are no enchantments in life, yet at the same time there are a thousand. Methodically, I live with great pleasure, deftness, horror. And my elbows are on the wood table. For twenty-five years, I've rested them on this wood. Wherever you go, there are gardens to look after. Let this angelica grow and let that other one be contained! Leave a tangle of raffia where one can find it if need be. Place a bunch of bamboo or reed stalks or a handful of hazel scions cut in fall or at winter's end against the walnut tree or in the crook of two branches. They form a sheaf and loose bundle. They've become a structured expanse in the garden where the most beautiful installations remain empty spaces, cleared plots, walkways with abandoned watering cans. The garden's only goal is abandon; it lives on abandon and thrives on the smallest opportunity to liberate itself and break through its imposed limits. Where is the garden? Between four walls or around the house? In the center or surrounding? In which garden am I sitting? In my garden. I am always in my garden, even when I'm not the gardener, and I don't need anything, neither to move nor to identify what's mine. It's my garden because I'm there, because I live in it for even just one second. And I part with it the next. I'm in the rose garden. I'm in the vegetable patch and in the future herb garden. I'm under the fig tree and under the ash. And I see what's faring poorly and what's doing just fine. I'm in the orchard of sweet grass, fallen among my spoils, completely stripped, rotten and shriveled among the rotten and shriveled apples. It's my garden because I can detect in it a number of signs that are so many proclamations of my next annihilation and at the same time of my negligence, decrepitude and even my happiness. It's my garden because it's within me and in spite of everything I have to give it up. All the signs slip suddenly from me because I neglected to refresh them and feed them. They dry out and crumble into dust. There is a dogwood cane wedged against the outside frame of the shed. In a white iron pail, there's a thin layer of sand from the Rhine. On the outer rim of a tiny transom, there's a dozen wedges of various kinds of wood, carefully stacked. A knife with no hilt, a pan with no handle. A pair of rusted pruning shears, outside of time or perfectly in step. There's also grass, boxwood leaves, dandelion and celandine flowers soaking in a white plastic basin, and a jump rope tied to the fork of the plum tree. There's the transom itself, and then, stepping a bit further back, the house with its high stone walls. To escape the exaltation of spring that was lost and more or less had strewn signs all about, you just have to wait for it to pass. To escape the fever of existence, you just have to wait for it—existence—to pass. The concoction steeping in the little white basin could be a witch's ancient brew that could cure life, and the jump rope could bind the hooves of a goat kid. The wooden wedges would wondrously balance a table standing on uneven terrain. Upon that stabilized table would stand four or five plates bearing a lattice of young, green asparagus spears or tens of cucumber slices. In the white iron pail, there's still a bit of sand that the gardener often mixes with dark soil. As for the knife with no hilt, it very improperly serves to cut young shoots as close to the root as possible. The transom provides a tiny source of supplementary light for the garden shed. The house thus composed appears livable and lived-in. The dogwood cane will possibly have a use one day. It was carved specifically, with patience and skill, for one use or another. You sometimes need to get several hundred miles away from the nerve center in order to read its signs. You have to be able to recognize a latent state of farsightedness. There is no garden without children.

Some days you neglect to observe the signs that appear on a calm sea. They will never be of any help. Looking up at the sky, a small quantity of circles try to gather and little is needed to keep them from orbiting. But it's clear right away that no curve becomes a circle, that even better, that there's an infinite braid and, better yet than an infinite braid, there is a marvelous spiral that extends or contracts without ever disappearing completely. But see how this image also disintegrates and disperses, and how the spring's outline subsides. You may perceive thus that these instantly perceivable signs find themselves spanning senseless frontiers, rolling out across the entire visible surface of the sea. Circles looping around or bits of shattered borders. But, while thought gets bogged down little by little into a muddle of curves, you see that the era of the curves is suddenly over and that the time of parallel lines begins. The wind's in our favor.

I can hear the man who's cutting up wood with a chainsaw. It's the Russian, the man with the dogs. His wife is a musician—a violinist for the opera. I resign myself to the wail of the chainsaw and abruptly the din disappears. I resign myself to the transistor radio, the idiotic songs and I put up with the stupidity of it. I'm bound to the man who whistles at night to call his cat and to the woman shouting in her garden. She who calls her neighbor has lost her husband, a sickly, oversensitive little Spaniard. I'm attached to others by lines so confused and so tangled that I can never tell who is who. From the ground floor comes the sound of a manhandled door, and from the road, the vibrations of a bus. The elasticity of the Earth's crust is evident and almost terrifying. I hear bells ringing. I smell smoke and can tell what's burning in one of the neighborhood gardens. They're going to bake the earth until it's as hard as glass. They destroy the dead leaves because they don't know what to do with them. They drive a car with no tailpipe. They chase insects around like a bat out of hell. They buzz round a turd. We summon children who neither come nor stay. We drain a balky sewer. It's heard, it's smelled. We fry potatoes. They're heard, they're smelled. The cat's under the tom. The Turk is dissatisfied with his satellite dish. I am, with my smells, face and vociferations, in the middle of what's moving, of what advances. No one should forget that they're part of the daily grind.

The kids, Louise and Marin, say that I must get to work when I withdraw to my office. The order's been given. The neighbors mustn't get any ideas. Just imagine, a man in the prime of life that you can find home at any hour of the day. And yet no one gives me a salary and I don't sell icons or precious wood statues. It's as if, without knowing it and since the day I was born, I've chosen to live off the generosity of others or on public charity. I withdraw to my office that's separated from the rest of the house only by a thin door. I sit—was that a mistake?—I take a sheet of paper. Let come what may in the period of time that I've given myself.

In summer, some perfectly fine plants need to be sacrificed to compost: rhubarb, black and red angelica, sunflower, fig, balsam. Even peach tree branches. In order to shade that pile. It's because he's living, this chap, and because he stinks atrociously when we forget him and he gets too hot. It took me some time to realize this. I thought that he was full of dead things like the stomach of a hung or drowned man, that he was harmless. He needs shade. He needs water. He needs light. He needs to move. He needs a soil peopled with earthworms and as cool as a mountain stream. He needs tea made of straw and coffee grounds. You'd generally think he doesn't exist or only in the form of a large pile. It's only when you turn him that you see him. It's only when you walk over him that you recognize him. Much like slippers, he's an intimate sign that ought to be hidden under a holly bush or behind tall sunflowers, like pushing slippers under the furniture, out of visitors' line of vision. A part of our life is stowed there—skins, peels, topographies of happiness and sometimes leftovers that even the cats won't deign to touch or sniff. Things of importance—like broad leaves of angelica, huge piles of maple leaves, grass of the most beautiful, splendiferous green, precious envelopes—calmly move toward their basest selves.

When making love, while kissing, my head spins and I rave, multiplying into two, thrashing around, with all hands on deck, into another body and taking the form of a two-headed animal, stunned by the hardness of the bone head that collides with mine, slamming again and again into a wall that the laws of pleasure are on the verge of breaking, dissolving. Pleasure is within a hand's or a foot's reach. Extravagant privileges are granted to the torso and limbs, and to the heart, limitless power. Mouth consumes mouth and eyes see beyond eyes. We take a dizzying shortcut leading only to more dizzying shortcuts. Each time, we copy down the nomenclature of each noble act. We clench our necks and haunches. We are batrachians on the perilous path to bliss, in amplexus. The large female holds the little male on her back. We disappear, lost with all hands, and perceive without surprise that that's what we've always sought. A murmur is the only possible tone for conversing: we're scared to wake the gods of old, tidal waves, earthquakes, fire rain. Together, flesh blazing open like flowers, blossoming, we're more vulnerable. The bed pitches like a rowboat. The earth favors us. She turns and turns us. The close-knit couple forever herds its flock of sheep between rolling waves.

We change our banners everyday. They come in all manner of shapes and colors, sometimes pierced by three gingko leaves, sometimes a chestnut branch. It matters to us to know where the wind comes from and where it's blowing. It's not as if we need to launch a hot-air balloon or charter a sailing ship right away, but rather out of interest for the movements that surround us, which make apples fall before they're ripe, which carry sounds, fumes and sand, which dry our sheets. These banners are points of reference. It's a question of knowing beyond a doubt whether it's the wind that's blowing or or us sliding down a slope. The clothespins that hold them more than suffice to do the job. In the event of a storm, we take them down and close the windows and doors.

The vegetable patch—simultaneously bright and gray, too humid and too dry—is in the middle of the garden, right in the middle of the yard. It's an islet of demanding and dour vegetables that require gallons of water. The growth of an ash tree, sending out its branches and roots, threatens it. The only things born into the world are those that we put, sowed and transplanted there, as well as a host of weeds—spontaneous and tough. This work consists of eliminating the undesirables and settling in their place those that we choose—in that way we are like an author. There's no work more thankless. To break even, a code was adopted. It consists of sowing turnips, radishes, carrots, cabbages and salsify in rows, more or less spaced out.

Next, it's necessary to attempt, day after day, to adhere to this initial approach. The design is primordial and almost immutable. Indeed, it's a hypnotic straightjacket. It foretells what will be the next godsend and appearance of the patch. The plot will pay off thanks to the branches of a mock-orange staked in the ground—because peas have no support, they need help to grow—as opposed to weeds that grow in clumps, rapidly becoming hordes of taproots or rhizomes. The vegetable patch demands organization at every level. It needs a panoply of tools that require constant upkeep, a good amount of water, a large fridge, a tidy larder, good cellars that are neither too humid nor too dark for tubers, jars for preserves, culinary artists and some excellent diners who won't mind the same thing over and over, or leftovers.

The rainwater cistern lies in front of the house, just beneath the terrace. It emits deep, faraway sounds. This void fills with water. It puts up with—on top of the weight of the water—the weight of children, visitors, our table and placesettings. We walk atop the void; our steps make it echo. It's better to imagine it deep and unfathomable like a well with which it shares just its subterranean nature. Peering into its mouth, apart from yourself, you can see the wall of the house with its roof poking out and the sky. It's a kind of treasure. Here, you reach it by the most direct route. You need to take off its cover, as if from a crypt, and toss in a bucket on the end of a rope. The chosen bucket is the heaviest possible, wide-mouthed and shallow. You cast it in like catching fish and pull it up full of black water whose opacity daylight diffuses. This way you can see the level drop before your eyes and lower toward the mire. The tank rings to announce it's empty. It empties to the rhythm of the water carriers, and its contents spill on the ground like rain, barely rerouting its natural runoff, scarcely less pure and less clear, clouded from rinsing off roofs. Water can only really be possessed, which is to say confined, for a short time. Water's in our favor. It washes tiles, rocks and tree leaves. It fades and ages us. When it seems still it flows fastest.

We rarely sow our seeds at the right time. It's always too early or too late. We were mistaken as to seeding or transplanting time. Or perhaps the seeds are missing. In any case, you may consider seedlings like gems we bury in little caches marked some way or another. If you're up to the task, it's best to draw up a precise plan on paper of all the caches in which the deposits were made. But a powerful and unavoidable gust scrambles the ciphers and plans. A multitude sprouts from the soil. The greenery is a sty with a stupefying logic: either it'll end in a soup or we'll be devoured. Even more perplexing, if you've a taste for puzzles, try combing the ground looking for roots. Down there, there's only the will to push in and grow out. Nothing is immobile. Everything goes, grows and spreads every which way. Nothing's on the road to ruin, but rather proliferates and prospers simultaneously. Bindweed climbs the walls and settles under and even in the walls themselves. It maps out a path, and its relics reveal the past, present and future route. Time lets it propagate, but it chooses its own way. It flows like water and does nothing but pass. And us—we catch the radishes before they escape, before they ripen, before they go to seed. And we gather fruit as we pass by.

It's customary to scale and gut our fish before eating them, under the pain of forgetting that it's the fish's soul itself that we covet, that we wrested from water and shadow, that we devour on white plates, in broad daylight. Indeed, it's the soul—what animates creatures, what makes them jump and move—that we relish with such great impunity, always afraid we'll swallow a bone. Under pain of forgetting that it's the soul that has this ineffable taste and this tender, firm consistency. It's the life and history of fish that we gobble up. So you have to have the courage to skin these fish totally—to rob them of their finery, their shimmering, to butcher them, starve them, to kidnap and murder them, finally consuming them. Therefore, I accept that my palms are profoundly impregnated with their scent, that my fingers are cut and scratched, and the walls of the kitchen are silver-plated with scales. I recognize that something ineluctable is produced, that something is lost, that there was asphyxiation, pain and true annihilation. It's good to know that the fish ended their lives in a kitchen sink—those that were fragrant, stubborn, curious, avoiding ridiculous lures only to fall into even cruder traps. And, capping the work of destruction, I leave the head on to cook with the body and be displayed on the table, eyes white and tongue torn out. We cannot—and it's all for the better—erase every trace of wrongdoing. The smell of fish becomes a trophy, much in the same way as a pheasant feather on a bird-hunter's hat or a necklace of teeth around a bear-hunter's throat. I don't know a keener, more exquisite and more acidic smell. The only thing left to do now is hang strings of swim bladder to block out the light and then to sleep peacefully amid the scent of soft fleece, iodine, and water mint.

When you decide to eat fowl or rabbit flesh, you must pluck or skin it yourself and empty the animal's stomach of its contents. Their stomachs contain traces of terrestrial lore. Once again, it's the jumping creature that interests us, it's the aging flesh that delights our palate, it's the whole—its stench, its living system, its entrails and the network of nerves beneath its skin. Chicken is tasty because it ate earthworms, baby shrews and cat vomit. And because it pecked out oats from the droppings of a well-fed horse. Also because its gizzard was always well stocked with pebbles, gravel and pottery shards, and because its kidneys always worked well. It's delicious because it rolled in dust to protect itself from parasites. It pleases us because it lived well. We enjoy its whole life in the flesh when we break the wishbone and hunt for the liver among the leaves of sage. Don't forget the rabbit's head after having stripped it of the skin that protected it from the cold, from bites and sun. It's the head we feast on first, having removed its long ears. Neither marrow nor brain nor tongue can be forgotten. We open the skull like breaking open a small safe, by unclenching its jaws.

Blood clouds the clear water.

There is a kind of utility in dipping your arm, then your whole body into the cloudy water of a river carrying white clay from the mountains. You can't live solely in clarity. It's not wrong to disappear from time to time—to try to dissolve into opacity, to be dissolved and for them to say look there he goes (dead) in the water and now he's there in the clouds' reflection. If he resurfaces, it's like a meteor blazing across the sky. You can finally proclaim that I'll disappear and disappear the following moment.

When you dip your right arm in water, milky from a ton of stagnant water, you're cut off from it. Your eye can no longer issue orders to your fingers that have to search for a toad or grass snake for themselves, trusting only their knowledge and ancient manipulations from children's books, trusting only that toads don't have teeth and grass snakes bite like old, toothless dogs.

Petting lizards, snakes and geckos as soon as the opportunity presents itself may be beneficial. Don't make fun of their movements, their lurching, their crests and their cool bodies. Rather, feel in their skin an unexplored parcel of the Earth's crust—a place we've never been able to reach no matter how hard we've tried. These animals are everywhere we're not. They occupy places we never could—the abandoned recesses, the far reaches, the crevices. They move shrewdly within countless tight spaces. They sleep horizontally, vertically or diagonally. They don't cry. They don't wail when dying, and slugs feed on their entrails. Nothing signals their presence on earth and no tocsin announces their death. The smallest failure costs them their lives. They know neither forgiveness nor absolution. Let's allow them to accede to that part of the world they've still never seen—to our skin, so dust and mites might commingle.

There comes a time when disgust at woodlice is no longer justified. You mustn't hesitate touching them—they who live in your house and under the bark of old trees, who knew the ancient ocean and whom the ocean abandoned in our caves where they became tiny little pigs. They multiply in the humidity that seeps from our walls, in our cozy steam, in our trash. They disgust us because we misunderstand them. There's a very simple method for getting used to their presence and even letting them into the kitchen and bedrooms. Just set about taking inventory of them, seeking first the largest that seem like miniature hedgehogs and roll into a ball when they are caught, then encircling the flocks and struggling to recognize each and every one in order to treat them each according to their personality. If some resemble hedgehogs, others have the appearance of bits of wool fluff or specks of dust. They are colored by what they eat and each one chooses its own food.

There comes a time when we eat watermelon. They are ultrasugary. I dreamt they came from the Ukraine, maybe from a shaded market in Odessa, with real black seeds that seem to have been thrown by the fistful into the darkest red flesh. The man who taught me how to choose them had bushy, severe eyebrows. He came from a village not far from Krakow. The only trip he ever took was the one that led him here, to the center of the world where every bump, every seed, every inch of soil is its own core. He was a joker. One day he offered me a belt with which, he insinuated, he had disciplined me so many times. I buckle it around my waist every time I have to chop wood.

We have to stay on good terms with rats. They dig deep burrows among us. And we have the temerity to claim to suffer from solitude! A rat in each hole and on each scrap of our memory. However, no rat has ever threatened a household that stays together or falls apart by magic. The rats that populate the underground ducts feed only on the surplus of our abundance that rains on their heads and falls in their mouths. They take what we leave—though they often take it before we've decided to leave it for them. They only feed on little morsels, as if they'd given themselves the task of reconstructing some sort of infinite puzzle that loses another piece every second of the day. Actually, they don't rip anything apart. They patch. And their bellies of patches serve as exchange points between the surface's light and darkness's depths. Their progress is like a train of thought that doubles back upon itself, withdrawing and advancing in zig-zags. A rat's fur is warmer and finer than the finest horse's coat and softer than a small child's hair. Their capacity to love is inexhaustible. While we want them dead or nonexistent, they love and respect us for what we are—extravagant and carefree. They never want to leave our side: everywhere in the shadows, their little eyes tell us so.

The dragon, my contemporary, told me that sentences are like magic spells. We compose them for better or worse, and we file them away thinking that they might be of use one day. Let's begin by speaking of nothing—we'll finish by saying everything.

The potatoes are cooking. Salt is stationed on the table. A thunderstorm threatens. The hours are short but time unlimited. Forks are placed next to knives. Spoons gleam in the drawer's half-light. Steam escapes through the window. Greenery covers the earth. Wisteria climbs the wash house chimney. It will soon be night; we cannot stop it. Then day will come; we cannot avoid it. Tomorrow will be Monday and the day after Tuesday, as it should be. Who taught me how to tell the days apart and add them up, one on top of the other? What threatens us apart from the length and lengthening of time? What's slow and fast, too short and too long, light and dark, and moves forward without ever turning back? It takes between thirty and forty minutes to bake a two-pound loaf of bread. In one whole day you can live an entire life. It's not clouds that advance, it's we who roll on. We have to trim hedges and harvest apples, but no one's making us. We have to choose the colors for the woodwork. We have to buy the color. We have to paint carefully. We have to live, but no one's making us. Soon the potatoes will be done and soon they'll be eaten.